This verse version of
Jack and the Beanstalk
is adapted from the one titled
The History of Mother Twaddle and the
Marvelous Achievements of her Son Jack,
written by B.A.T.
that appeared in London in 1807,
published by J. Harris,
corner of St. Paul's Churchyard.

The assistance of the
Osborne Collection of the Toronto Public Library
is gratefully acknowledged.

For another Jack

Clarion Books
a Houghton Mifflin Company imprint
215 Park Avenue South, New York, NY 10003
Copyright © 1974 by Paul Galdone

Printed in the USA

LIBRARY OF CONGRESS CATALOGING IN PUBLICATION DATA

Main entry under title: Jack and the beanstalk.
SUMMARY: Jack climbs the great beanstalk that grows from the bean he bought and confronts a
giant at the top.
   A verse version of Jack and the beanstalk, originally titled the history of Mother Twaddle and the
marvelous achievements of her son Jack, written by B.A.T. and published in 1807 by J. Harris, London.
   [1. Folklore.   2. Fairy tales.   3. Stories in rhyme]   I. Galdone, Paul, illus.
II. B.A.T.   III. T., B.A.   IV. The history of Mother Twaddle and the marvelous achievements of
her son Jack.

PZ8.1.H664 1974   398.2'1'0942   73-9726
ISBN: 0-395-28801-0   Paperback ISBN: 0-89919-085-5

(Previously published by The Seabury Press in hardcover under ISBN: 0-8164-3112-4,
  and titled The History of Mother Twaddle and the Marvelous Achievements of her Son Jack)

WOZ 20 19 18

JACK
and the
BEANSTALK

Paul Galdone

CLARION BOOKS
NEW YORK

As Old Mother Twaddle
Was sweeping her floor,
She found a new sixpence
Under the door.
And as she surveyed it
With exquisite pleasure,
She called her son Jack
To look at her treasure.

"I will comb thee, and wash thee,
  And make thee quite spruce.
Thou shalt go to the fair
  And buy us a goose.
For of all the good things,
  I vow and protest,
A fat, tasty goose
  Is the thing I love best."

When Old Mother Twaddle
   Had sent Jack to the fair,
She hastened with onions
   And sage to prepare
A savory stuffing
   For the delicate treat,
And thought with what glee
   Of the tidbits she'd eat.

When Jack reached the fair
   And round him was staring
A peddler cried out,
   "Buy this bean for a farthing.
It possesses such virtues
   That sure as a gun,
Tomorrow it will grow
   Near as high as the sun!"

Jack bought it for sixpence
 Then went to his Mother,
Who at sight of the bean
 Made a terrible pother.
She gave him a scolding
 And slapped both his hands,
For having presumed
 Not to mind her commands.

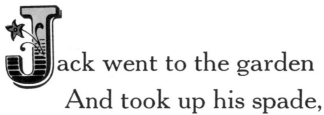ack went to the garden
    And took up his spade,
Then put the rare bean
    In the hole he had made,
Expecting to find
    This great wonder of wonders
As tall as a tree
    To make up for his blunders.

ext morning Jack rose
　　To view the large bean,
When to his surprise,
　　E'en the top was not seen!
It made a long ladder
　　As strong as a rope,
And Jack soon climbed on high
　　Full of joy and of hope.

He knocked at the door
    Of a very grand place;
A damsel came to it
    With a cap all of lace.
"Oh! Pray go from hence!"
    Cried this maid in a fright,
"For a giant lives here,
    And he'll eat you this night!"

Jack begged to come in
    With so winning an air
That she promised to hide him
    And pointed out where.
He no sooner had hidden
    Than the door opened wide,
And in stalked the Giant
    With a very long stride.

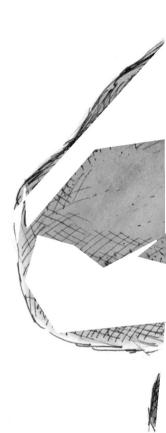

Then the Monster roared out,
"Fe, fi, fo, fan!
I smell the breath
Of an Englishman!
If he be alive,
Or if he be dead,
I'll grind his bones
To make my bread!"

"Oh wait, my dear Giant,
    First drink some strong wine,
Then on that dainty
    You may afterwards dine."
He seized a large cup
    And tippled so deep,
Then he tumbled down flat
    And fell fast asleep.

oon as Jack saw him fall,
   He crept from the bed,
Then snatched a large knife
   And chopped off his head.
Thus he killed this great man,
   As he loudly did snore,
And never again
   Was a Giant seen more.

Jack sent for his Mother
    To come up and dine,
With a promise of goose
    And a bottle of wine.
And as she did eat it
    With excessive delight,
She approved of his bargain
    And said he'd done right.

Jack sent for a parson,
    As he had a great mind
To marry the damsel,
    Who was willing and kind.
The Parson came soon
    And made her Jack's Wife,
And they lived very happy
    To the end of their life.

Here Jack, and his Wife,
And his Mother are seen
All dancing a jig
Round the wonderful bean.